W9-AHY-754

Runaway Alphabet

Written by Kari-Lynn Winters

Illustrated by Ben Frey

First published in 2010 by Simply Read Books
www.simplyreadbooks.com

Text Copyright © 2010 Kari-Lynn Winters
Illustrations Copyright © 2010 Ben Frey

For my childhood snow buddies—Sheena, Paula, Dawn, Jill,
and Ken. Special thanks to the educators who supported
me and this book, particularly Marilyn, Amanda, Kim,
Karen, Cheryl, Meghan, Morgan, and Emmanuel. – KLW

To Mom, Dad, Beth, Sean, and Dan—the most inspiring
family that anyone could ever ask for. – Ben

All rights reserved. No part of this publication may be reproduced,
stored in a retrieval system, or transmitted, in any form or by any
means, electronic, mechanical, photocopying, recording or otherwise,
without the written permission of the publisher. The publisher does
not have any control over and does not assume any responsibility for
author or third-party websites or their content.

Library and Archives Canada Cataloguing in Publication

Winters, Kari-Lynn, 1969-
    Runaway alphabet / written by Kari-Lynn Winters ; illustrated
by Ben Frey.

ISBN 978-1-897476-33-8

    1. English language--Alphabet--Juvenile fiction. 2. English
language--
Phonetics--Juvenile fiction. 3. Alphabet books. I. Frey, Ben, 1978- II.
Title.

PS8645.I58R85 2009   j428.1'3   C2009-905573-2

We gratefully acknowledge for their financial support of our publishing
program the Canada Council for the Arts, the BC Arts Council, and
the Government of Canada through the Book Publishing Industry
Development Program (BPIDP).

Book design by Steedman Design

10 9 8 7 6 5 4 3 2 1

Manufactured by Hung Hing Printing Group
Manufactured in Shenzhen, Guangdong, China, in November 2009
Job # SR0909001

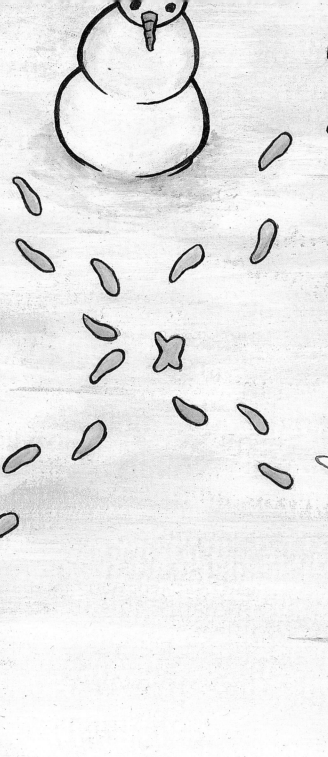

Introduction

Research shows that reading to and with children, and playing with the sounds of language, foster children's growth in language and literacy. Alphabet books incorporate both of these activities and can play an important role in young children's literacy development. Traditional alphabet books typically focus on words that begin with particular letters, such as "a for apple and alligator." Sometimes alphabet books are themed, such as an animal alphabet or a west-coast alphabet. Other alphabet books use the letters of the alphabet in alliteration, such as "Amazing aardvarks always admire armadillos."

Kari-Lynn Winters and Ben Frey have created a unique alphabet book. *Runaway Alphabet* differs from traditional alphabet books in two ways: first, the sounds commonly associated with letters represent sounds made by people or objects, such as "*d-d-ddd-d*" for the sound of drums and "*g-g-g-g*" for the sound Pa makes when gulping down his coffee; second, these letter-sound relationships are interwoven within a story.

We invite you to read and enjoy *Runaway Alphabet* with your children and, after shared reading or hearing the enclosed CD several times, encourage them to chime in, and then, when ready, to try reading on their own. In this way, *Runaway Alphabet* can be a stepping-stone on the path to literacy.

Marilyn Chapman, PhD

Professor, Language and Literacy Education
Director, Institute for Early Childhood Education and Research
The University of British Columbia, Vancouver, BC

Bumpity bump!

Nan likes the bouncy
bus ride. Pa tries to read.
But reading
makes him dizzy.

At the carnival Pa shivers.
"It's c-c-cold. Maybe some
food will warm us up."

"Pa, listen to
the drums!"

**d-d-ddd-d.
d-d-ddd-d.**

"**e!**" Pa cries. "I spilt mustard on my jacket."

Nan doesn't hear him. She is marching after the drummers.

ff-ff-ff.

Pa quickly wipes up
his mess and...

"g-g-g-g."

He gulps down his coffee,
then hurries after Nan.

"**hhh-hhh-hhh,**" Pa pants.

"**i-i-i!**" He cringes.
"The other players are so big."

"**mmm,**" says Nan as she takes off the skates. "Something smells yummy."

Pa struggles, trapped between the players.

p-p-p, sputters the popcorn popper.

"q-q-q-q-q."

Nan munches the popcorn.
"What should I do next?"
Pa looks for Nan.
"What will she do next?" he wonders.

rrrrrr, rumbles the snowmobile that takes people up the mountain. Nan grabs a tube and hops on.

Pa tries to catch up
with her, but oops!

SSSSSS.

Nan slides down the slope.
"Look at me!"

Pa can't hear her.
He has a carrot in his ear!

VVVVVVV, hums the lift. Nan runs towards it.

"Wait for me!" calls Pa.

XXXX.
Pa's boots scrape the icy snow.
He catches the back of Nan's toboggan—just in time.
"Pa! You've finally caught up!"

"yyyyyyy!" cheer Nan and Pa as they slide down the slope.